The Sword of Cortés

by Rob Kidd
Illustrated by Jean-Paul Orpinas

Based on the earlier life of the character, Jack Sparrow,
created for the theatrical motion picture,
"Pirates of the Caribbean: The Curse of the Black Pearl"
Screen Story by Ted Elliott & Terry Rossio and Stuart Beattie and Jay Wolpert,
Screenplay by Ted Elliott & Terry Rossio,
and characters created for the theatrical motion pictures
"Pirates of the Caribbean: Dead Man's Chest" and
"Pirates of the Caribbean: At World's End"
written by Ted Elliott & Terry Rossio

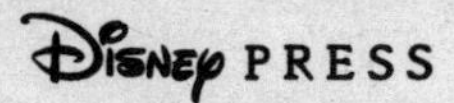

New York

Printed in the United States of America

First Edition
3 5 7 9 10 8 6 4

Library of Congress Catalog Card Number 2006905276

ISBN 1-4231-0061-1
DisneyPirates.Com

The Sword of Cortés

CHAPTER ONE

Jack Sparrow's mates—the fearless crew of the mighty *Barnacle*—had finally been shaken. They'd been searching so long for the Sword of Cortés, a weapon with unearthly power, that they had lost track of time. Had it been days, weeks, or months since they'd first set out on their quest and encountered sea beasts, cursed pirates, and the cunning and vicious merfolk? No one could remember exactly, but they knew it had felt like a long and tiring journey.

They had arrived on Isla Fortuna only that morning. They discovered that the notorious pirate Left-Foot Louis was in possession of the Sword. He had used its power to cause all of the honest people of Isla Fortuna to vanish. In just a few hours, the crew had defeated the vicious pirate and finally procured from him their prize. The Sword was in their hands now, reunited with its scabbard.

They knew from legend that when the two charmed parts of the weapon were joined and an ancient incantation read, the Sword would become imbued with godlike power.

Jack Sparrow had done all that. But when he waved the Sword and spouted off the first few magical spells that came to mind, nothing happened. He wasn't able to make anything disappear or transform, things he thought a magic sword should be able to do easily. In fact, the Sword seemed less powerful now than it ever had. Something was wrong.

Very wrong.

Jack was frustrated. He was about to toss the Sword away, but the horrified looks on the faces of his crew told him that he should reconsider. A second later, Jack realized they were looking at something *behind* him. He whirled around and saw—well, he wasn't quite sure what it was.

Jack's first mate, Arabella, was quick to fill him in.

"Jack," she said, "don't ye realize what's happened? The pirates' stories lacked a wee detail. The incantation ye read brought back the Sword's owner! This is the spirit of Hernán Cortés, risen from the dead!"

Jack sized up the phantom. Was Arabella

sure he had *risen* from the dead? The chap still looked pretty un-alive to Jack. The pale, sallow man was clad in old Spanish armor. The stench of rot hung around him. Jack waved his hand in front of his face and coughed to vanquish the smell, but it didn't work. Cortés was one stinky conquistador. His glowing red eyes glared at Jack.

Then Jack did what any good adventure-seeking captain would do. He stepped up to Cortés and introduced himself.

"Well, hello there, mate," Jack said, extending his hand. "Captain Jack Sparrow. How very nice to meet you."

Apart from Cortés's chest, which heaved and fell heavily (Jack thought this rather odd for a dead—or *undead*—guy), Cortés did not move. His breath stank like a barrel of rotten fish.

Jack smiled uncomfortably, coughed, and

dropped his arm. "So, mate, I suspect you've materialized here, from wherever it is you dead people go, in order to get the Sword back, eh?"

Cortés leaned forward, attempting to bow. This appeared to be quite difficult for him. His armor creaked and his bones seemed to crack.

"The Sword," Cortés said in thickly accented English, "is now yours. You read the incantation. *You* invoked its power."

The crew of the *Barnacle* was shocked—and impressed—that Jack was so at ease talking to a dead fellow.

"So, then," Jack said, "why are you here? A genie from the bottle or something like that? Just come along for the ride? Stick by ye ol' sword whenever it may be imbued with godlike power? Oh, wait, let me correct myself, ye ol' sword that is *supposed* to have *been* imbued with godlike power." Jack tapped the blade with his index finger. "Your little metal stick doesn't seem to be doing much of anything right now."

"I am here, boy," Cortés said in a grave voice, clearly trying to put Jack in his place, "to teach you how to use this weapon."

Jack's eyes brightened and he turned to his crew, smiling broadly. The crew was much less at ease with the current situation than their captain.

Jack cleared his throat and clapped his hands together. "So, when do my lessons begin?"

Cortés stepped forward, his armor grating and squeaking.

"Now," he answered.

There was a long pause. Cortés did not say anything more. Jack raised an eyebrow.

"Want to give me a little more instruction

than that, mate?" Jack asked. Behind his hand, he whispered to Arabella, "Now we know why he was a conquistador and not a schoolteacher in his former life."

"Take the Sword and point it toward the port's docks," Cortés told him.

From the hilltop graveyard where they stood, Jack had a clear view of the docks below. He lifted the Sword and pointed it at the dock farthest from where they had moored the *Barnacle*. An unbelievably powerful current of energy flowed through Jack's body and out through the Sword. Instantly, it blew the empty dock out of the water.

"Whoa!" was all Jack could muster.

He examined the blade closely. It was smoking and smelled of sulfur. He could feel heat radiating from it onto his face.

Cortés smiled.

Jack quickly whirled around and pointed

the Sword at Constance, the mangy, obnoxious cat that Jack's crewmate, Jean, claimed was his sister under a curse.

"Begone!" Jack shouted.

"Constance!" Jean cried out in horror.

But nothing happened. Constance just hissed at Jack, stretched, and yawned. Then she sat down and curled her twitching tail around her.

"I knew it wouldn't work, or else I wouldn't have tried it," Jack said quietly to Jean. He hoped he sounded convincing.

Jean wasn't buying it. He scowled at Jack and ran to Constance, gathering the nasty, matted cat up in his arms.

Just then, Cortés stepped up behind Jack. Cortés placed his slimy, decaying hands over Jack's and gripped the Sword with him.

"Do you think we can use this sword to clean you up a bit, mate? Maybe just to get rid of that awful smell?" Jack asked.

Cortés did not seem to be bothered by Jack's quips. He extended Jack's arms, pointing the Sword toward the sea. Another rush of energy flowed through Jack. A haze of vapor began to rise off the sea. It rapidly became thicker. Within seconds, the water along the entire coast of Isla Fortuna was violently boiling.

Cortés stepped away from Jack, smiling smugly, and the sea simmered down.

Then, Cortés stepped up to Jack again, holding the Sword together with him once more. Jack looked out at the turquoise Caribbean. The *Cutlass*! In all the excitement, Jack had shoved to the back of his mind that despite the fact that the pirate himself was gone, Left-Foot Louis's ship and crew were still docked right off the island.

Cortés positioned Jack's arms—and the Sword—so that they were directly in line with the *Cutlass.* The huge pirate ship with its signature crimson Jolly Roger shimmered on the sea. Then with a quick blink, the ship vanished.

"Guess that threat is over with," Jack said flatly.

His crew was in awe.

"Neither the ship, nor the crew, will interfere with you any longer," Cortés said.

Jack shifted uncomfortably, unsettled by the fact that Cortés had made an entire ship and its crew disappear. And all the while, Jack had been holding the mystical sword.

Cortés stepped away from Jack again.

Jack wiped Cortés's slimy grime from his hands and stared at the Sword in awe. He looked at Cortés, who was still smiling, then turned his attention back to the Sword, which glowed with a waning power, the way a hot iron would as it cooled. Finally, Jack turned to his crewmates. Their expressions ranged from uneasy to terrified. Could no one share in his enthusiasm? Jack rolled his eyes and stomped over to his trusted crew, who were waiting for him at the foot of the hill.

Tumen, a Mayan sailor, looked particularly troubled.

"Tumen!" Jack said, smiling. He slapped the young sailor on the back. "Look alive, mate! What's eating at you?"

"I'm just not feeling very well," Tumen said.

"He does look pale," Arabella said, touching Tumen's forehead. "And he has a bit of a fever, too."

"Well, never fear, Tumen, mate," Jack

said. "Once I learn to properly wield this sword, I'll make you right as rain."

"Jack," Tumen said, shaking his head and clearly straining to speak, "I don't trust this sword."

"Well, you didn't seem to have any trust issues *prior* to discovering it."

"That was before I saw what she could do," Tumen urged. "This type of power is dangerous. And what's worse is . . . Cortés." Tumen looked over at the ghastly figure and shuddered. "He scourged the Yucatán before moving inland to defeat the Aztecs. This sword had a part in that slaughter."

"But we said we'd take the Sword and harness its power for different purposes. To free ourselves—to free the Caribbean—from pirates and corrupt politicos and all sorts of other ne'er-do-wells," Jack said, waving his hand dismissively.

"I have a different view now," Tumen said, slumping against a nearby tree to support himself.

"As do I," Fitzwilliam P. Dalton III, the aristocratic runaway, chimed in. Seeing the corrosive conquistador in the flesh—or lack thereof—was really giving the crew a very different perspective. "Cortés slaughtered an entire empire. He could have very well used that sword to do it. Families, Jack. Mothers, fathers, *children*. Let's think about this rationally."

"Oh, you aristos and your rational behavior! 'Rational' this and 'rational' that," Jack said, waving the blade carelessly. "Fitzy, there is nothing remotely rational about this here sword. And I am convinced that I can make this work to our benefit. It might have made a lot of bad things happen in the past, but it doesn't have to *be* bad."

The crew members stood silent, clearly united against Jack. Despite their earlier enthusiasm, now that they had seen what the Sword could do, none of the crew wanted its full power unleashed.

Jack sneered.

"You're either with me on this, or you're against me," Jack said.

The crew, even Constance, still stood united in their defiance.

"Very well, then," Jack said. Turning his back on his crew, he started back toward Cortés.

CHAPTER TWO

Jack found Cortés waiting patiently at the top of the hillside graveyard.

"Welcome back."

"What say we cut the formalities and just get this business done with, savvy?" Jack said.

"The first rule is to respect your elders," Cortés answered. "And I am certainly your elder, by hundreds of years."

Jack remembered Arabella saying that

Cortés died in the middle of the sixteenth century. That would make him very old, indeed. More than two hundred years older than Jack . . . if you counted all the years the conquistador spent dead in between.

"Well, then, old man, may I beg you to please guide me in the ways of this so-very-mystical sword?" Jack asked sarcastically. "Respectful enough for you?"

Jack handed the Sword over to Cortés.

"*Much* better," Cortés said, swishing the Sword before him. Sparks flew from the blade, and the air that it cut seemed to take on an iridescent glow.

Jack looked down the hill, where his crew waited and watched. Jack shot them an arrogant glance.

"Now, take the Sword," Cortés said.

Jack reached out for it, but Cortés quickly pulled it away.

"Not like that," Cortés said. Then he drove the tip of the Sword into the ground. "Now, take it. But don't move from where you are."

"With all due respect, Cortsy, that sword is a good three yards away from me. How am I supposed to retrieve it from way back yonder?"

"Use its power. Concentrate and call it to you."

"Call it to me?" Jack said. "Here-swordy-swordy-swordy!"

"No! Call it with your *mind*. Call it with your *soul*," Cortés said.

Jack gave Cortés a dubious glance, then redirected his attention to the Sword.

"Concentrate," Cortés told him.

Jack looked at the Sword. He thought about all the things he could do with it. He could be the captain of his own ship. A *real* ship, not like the *Barnacle*. He could rule his own island. Sail the Seven Seas—and rule them, too. He would be free of all the constraints placed upon him. He'd answer to no one but himself.

As Jack thought about all these things, the Sword slowly rose from the ground and floated into his hand. Jack gripped the Sword and felt a tingle of energy emanate from its hilt. He smiled.

"Very good," Cortés said.

"Thank you," Jack replied, bowing. "You know, I really have always been very good at things like this—levitating objects and such. I once juggled a scallop and a sea cucumber using nothing more than my breath and my willpower."

"Did you?" Cortés said skeptically.

Jack squirmed awkwardly. "Yes, well, anyway, back to this here sword." He held it out to the sea and willed a fleet of ships to appear—a fleet he would command. But nothing happened. Cortés stepped up to him once again.

"You've not yet perfected the art. Point the blade toward that valley in the distance."

"Which one, mate? This island is full of hills and dales. Come on, get with it. Specifics. We need specifics," Jack said.

"Any one of them will do," Cortés replied, and Jack could hear a note of agitation in his voice. Jack felt proud. It wasn't every mate who could tick off the undead.

Jack waved the Sword before him more dramatically than he probably needed to. Then he pointed it at a valley near the center of the island. The valley began to shimmer. Before Jack's eyes, it was suddenly filled with a roaring current of water. He'd created a river from nothing! Well, nothing but thin air and the magic of a legendary sword.

What else could he do? Jack pointed the Sword at the river, and willed it to turn red. But nothing happened. He waved the Sword back and forth, willing treasure to fall from the sky and jewels to spring from the ground. Still nothing. He pointed the Sword at his crew, which, even from a distance was noticeably terrified to be in its line of fire. Jack willed them to cooperate with him, but they did not move from their place at the foot of the hill.

With every failure, Jack became more frustrated.

"Seems this here sword only works when you're telling me what to do with it, mate," Jack said, handing the Sword back to Cortés. "So, why don't you just play with the landscape on your own? A river here, a rainbow there, maybe a tea shop down in the town square for the tourists."

Cortés's red eyes glowed like hot coals. He was clearly angered, and for the first time Jack felt a twinge of fear. Cortés held the Sword above his head and howled an unearthly scream that shook the very ground beneath Jack's feet.

Above Cortés's head, the sky soon began to churn with a thick cover of roiling black clouds. There was a crack of thunder followed by a flood of rain. Then the humid heat of the Caribbean afternoon was swept away by a bitterly cold wind. Jack had never felt so chilled in his life.

He looked up, and what he saw truly amazed him. Huge white flakes cascaded from the sky. The Sword of Cortés had caused it to snow—right there in the Caribbean.

Cortés smiled smugly once more. "So, how do you like the new landscape?" he asked. Jack did not respond, he was clearly stunned. "Your first lesson is over," Cortés continued. "In fact, this first lesson will also be your last. You now know all you need to know."

But Jack was not having it. He clearly did not, in fact, have the training he needed in order to properly work the Sword. What was this Cortés mate trying to pull?

"Jack!" Jean called out, running up the hill toward his captain. His crewmates were right behind him, their teeth chattering. They were not prepared for weather like this, especially on an island where the temperature rarely dropped below scorching.

Jack casually pointed the Sword toward the sky and commanded the snow to stop falling, but to no avail. Would he ever

master this sword? Especially now that Cortés was giving up on training him?

"Jack, I'm worried about Tumen. He's getting worse," Jean said.

Jack looked over at Tumen, who was supported on either arm by Arabella and Fitzwilliam. He looked only a shade healthier than Cortés. The cold and snow could not be good for such a sick sailor.

"We need to take him back to town," Arabella said. "Jack, look at him. He's near death with whatever it is that's afflicting him. We need to get him into warm blankets and near a fire and some shelter. And that goes for the rest of us, too. Will ye be joining us? Or is yer lesson that much more important than yer crew?"

"I resent that," Jack said. "Go on, I will be there shortly."

"Jack," Arabella said, "not long ago ye

convinced me not to do something I'd regret, not to become someone—some*thing*—I didn't want to become.* I only hope I can convince ye of the same thing. Just, please, be careful. I care for ye, Jack. We *all* care for ye." She kissed him on the cheek, gathered up the rest of the crew, and set off in search of shelter in the town below.

Jack hesitated for a moment, then turned back to Cortés.

"Okay, mate, now listen. I know that I can't use this sword just yet, despite what you say. So I'm asking you, about as kind as Jack Sparrow knows how, to show me how to use it."

"I can make you a master of the Sword," Cortés told him.

"So, what are you waiting for?" Jack said.

*See our last installment, Vol. 3: *The Pirate Chase*, when Jack convinced Arabella not to kill Left-Foot Louis.

"But on a condition . . ."

"*Of course* it's on a condition. What in the bloody Caribbean is not done on *some* condition or other? And what is said condition, señor?"

"Retrieve for me the eye of the man who last wielded this sword. I want the stone eye that belonged to the pirate Stone-Eyed Sam."

CHAPTER THREE

Jack felt blood rush to his head. Just weeks before, he had been held at the mercy of a race of creatures called merfolk—women who were half human and half, well, fish-things. Jack managed to strike a deal with the Scaly Tails, as he called them: he would be free to leave their lair, but must eventually return and turn over to them his greatest treasure. It was only after he agreed to these terms that Jack realized what his greatest treasure was—his freedom. Ironically, Jack had been set free on the condition that he would one day return to the merfolk as their captive or, presumably, be *taken* prisoner.

And there was one more detail. At the time of his encounter with the merfolk, Jack had been in possession of the eye of the pirate Stone-Eyed Sam. However, before the merfolk released him, they had asked for collateral. To Jack, the eye didn't seem like much—nothing more than a memento of his first adventure with the *Barnacle*'s crew. But the merfolk had seemed mighty happy to have it.* And now Cortés wanted it, too.

"Now where would I find something as strange and obscure as a dead pirate's stone eye?" Jack asked Cortés, brushing some

*Jack's encounter with the merfolk took place back in Vol. 2: *The Siren Song*.

snow from his shoulders, trying to play it cool.

"I think you know," Cortés replied.

So much for fooling this guy. Now Jack saw his dilemma. He had to somehow get back to the merfolk to reclaim the eye. But at the same time, he needed to figure out a way to avoid again becoming their prisoner. And how would he do that?

Jack decided not to worry about it until he was face-to-face with the Scaly Tails. He would find a way out of the situation—and he'd figure it out when he needed to. Right now, he had bigger fish to fry—so to speak.

"Fine, then. I'll go on a quest to retrieve this eye. But I'm going to need that there sword—what sometimes glows and does little things like make it snow in the Caribbean and create rivers from valleys and such."

"I had no intention of sending you without it," Cortés answered.

"Brilliant. I'll just take this sword, then, gather my crew, and we'll be on our way."

"No," Cortés said. "You are to take no one with you on this mission. It is something you must do alone. We cannot risk anyone interfering with our plans."

"'Our' plans?" Jack asked. "Sorry, mate, but this is *your* plan, not mine."

"It's yours, as well. That is, if you want to wield the full power of the Sword."

"I can't say that I am entirely comfortable with this arrangement. After all, what is a captain without his crew? How is he to sail his ship?" Jack asked.

"You go alone, or the Sword—and all its power—will stay here," Cortés said. "He who possesses this sword needs no crew."

Cortés handed Jack the Sword and told

him to point it toward the *Barnacle*, which was safely docked on the unscathed side of the port. The little boat rocked on the waves. It was covered by a thin blanket of snow.

"Here you go again telling me what to do with this here sword," Jack snapped at Cortés. "One of these days I'm going to tell you what *you* can do with it!"

"Just do as I say. You won't regret it."

Jack lifted the Sword and pointed it at his little fishing boat. And a fishing boat is all it really was—no matter how much he wanted to believe it was a great ship. His crewmate Fitzwilliam never missed an opportunity to remind Jack of that fact.

But Jack had come to love that boat. And so he was not only shocked and shaken, but also hit with a great pang of grief, when both the bow and the stern began to split. The crack made its way up the center of the *Barnacle*, and finally the boat began to break in two. Bits of wood from the splintered deck flew through the air. Then, a series of blasts shook the sea. A cloud of smoke rose up around the docks where the boat had been moored.

What have I done? Jack wondered with shock and regret.

Far below in the snow-covered town, Arabella and Fitzwilliam ran from the inn where they'd taken shelter. They strained to see what had happened to their boat. And so did Jack.

Then the cloud of dust and smoke began to clear. Through the veil of the snowfall, the *Barnacle* emerged. But it was no longer a wee fishing boat. It had been completely transformed.

Jack stared out at the ship and smiled

proudly. GRAND BARNACLE was now painted across its broadside. The ship was so large it barely fit in the dock. It had become a glorious war vessel, fit with multiple decks and sails and cannons . . . cannons upon cannons upon cannons!

"It suits you well, Jack Sparrow," Cortés said.

Jack continued to stare, at a loss for words.

Nearly.

"But if I'd have had difficulty sailing a *boat* on my own, how in the name of all that's blessed and blasted am I going to sail a *ship*?" he asked, getting a hold of himself.

Cortés took the blade from Jack once again and tapped him on the shoulder with it. Jack felt a shock of energy run through him, stronger than any of the previous jolts from the Sword.

"Now," Cortés said, "you have everything you need."

Jack held the Sword up to the *Grand Barnacle* once more, and the huge sails of what was now the greatest warship ever to sail the Caribbean unfurled.

CHAPTER FOUR

Jack felt a rush of high energy as he raced down the snowy hillside toward Isla Fortuna's small town of Puerto San Judas. Down on the beaches, it was hard to tell where the white sand ended and the snow began. During his time as a stowaway, Jack had spent winter in colder places, but he had never seen a snowfall like this. It looked strange in the tropical setting. Instead of blanketing pines and barren oaks, the snow

covering was piled on palm fronds and coconut groves. The surf near the shore was filled with chunks of icy slush. But only fifty feet out to sea, the thick cloud cover ended abruptly and the hot Caribbean sun shone down on the turquoise water.

The town square of Puerto San Judas looked like something out of Charles Dickens—that is, if Dickens had written stories about the Caribbean. At the far end of the town, near the docks, the chimney of the small inn spewed smoke. Arabella and Fitzwilliam were standing outside, wrapped in blankets and staring in wonder at the *Grand Barnacle*. Jack had come down from the hill. He did not intend to stop and speak to them as he walked through the town toward the great ship. But Arabella had a way of catching anyone's ear, especially Jack's.

"So, that there's our ship, eh?" she asked Jack as he walked past the inn.

"If you don't mind, milady, it's *my* ship, *my* sword, *my* adventure," Jack answered flatly, continuing his walk toward the *Grand Barnacle*.

Arabella grabbed Jack by the arm and slapped him square across the face.

Jack snarled and rubbed his cheek. "I didn't deserve that."

"Oh, yes, ye did, Jack. Ye deserve that and more," Arabella said. "I've had about enough of ye. A member of yer crew is *dying* and yer off hopping onto bedeviled ships and sailing away. Yer not the Jack we know, the Jack who—for whatever forsaken reason—we all trust."

"Oh, I don't know what all this fuss is about," Jack said. "I told you that you are either in this with me or you're not. You chose your side. So now I'll bid you adieu, farewell, ciao, sayonara, good-bye, and good riddance!"

"And how, pray tell, do you intend to sail a vessel such as the *Grand Barnacle* on your own?" Fitzwilliam asked.

"I have my ways, mate," Jack answered.

"It is impossible," Fitzwilliam responded. "A ship like that would require a crew of hundreds. You cannot do it on your own."

"Oh, no?" Jack said. "Watch me."

Jack pointed the Sword at the *Grand Barnacle* and the gangplank lowered.

"Ta for now," Jack said as he ascended the plank. "I'll be seeing you soon. Don't go anywhere in the meantime. Oh, wait, that's right. You *can't* go anywhere. There's not a boat left in the port."

"You will regret your leaving us, Jack Sparrow," Fitzwilliam said, shaking his hand up at the boat.

"I regret nothing, ever," Jack said as he pointed the Sword at the gangplank to lift it. Then he waved the Sword toward the lines and anchor that held the great ship at dock. Both the lines and the anchor snapped back toward the ship, like snakes recoiling from fire. The *Grand Barnacle* slowly moved away from the snowy port and into the sunny heat of the Caribbean Sea. Jack waved his bandanna mockingly at Fitzwilliam and Arabella as the ship pulled out. And as the figures of his land-bound crew grew smaller and smaller, and finally disappeared in the distance, Jack Sparrow fought to quell any regrets he might have.

Jack found sailing the *Grand Barnacle* a breeze, if a little lonely. He discovered he could make the ship spin just by whirling the Sword in the air above his head. He could steer it, just by pointing the Sword in the direction he wished to sail. He could even adjust the rigging and raise and lower the sails, simply by waving the Sword. Sailing such a big ship alone *should* have been impossible—and "impossible" was just the sort of feat Jack loved. But none of this was very challenging at all.

When he grew tired from the hot sun, he waved the Sword at the clear sky overhead and willed some clouds to roll in. When he grew hungry, he waved the Sword at the sea and bushels of crabs sprang out of the water and onto the ship's upper decks. By waving it again, they were prepared exactly as Jack liked them—steamed and buttered.

Still, the silence was profound. Jack fought his feelings, but found it difficult. He wished Arabella were there to make smart remarks. Or that Tumen and Jean were chasing that cursed cat Constance around the deck. He even wished Fitzwilliam was onboard to argue with him about the course he was charting.

Which was another matter to consider—what course *was* he charting? Isla Sirena, where the merfolk dwelled, resided not in the Caribbean, but in Davy Jones's locker—a place few knew about firsthand, but the sailors' stories did not make it sound pleasant. The island emerged out from the dark depths of Jones's realm only occasionally and, it seemed to Jack, with no rhyme or reason. How was he supposed to find an island from another realm?

"Well," Jack said to himself, "the Scaly Tails found me easily enough last time. I suppose the best thing to do is sail to a place where there is no land in sight and just wait. Easier for an island to drop in, when there's not an obstacle in the way," Jack reasoned.

Jack pointed the Sword at the sails, and a gust of wind filled them. The *Grand Barnacle* sped far out into the Caribbean waters. After some time, Jack found himself in a part of the Caribbean Sea where he could see no land—not the slightest indication of an island—in any direction.

"Guess I'll just wait here, then," Jack said. He walked over to the broadside of the huge ship and stared out to the sea. It was calm, disrupted only by fish breaking the surface now and then. Jack heard nothing but the lapping of the waves and the occasional caw of a seabird. The sounds of the sea and the rocking of the boat were so relaxing that Jack's eyelids grew heavy, and he found it difficult to fight sleep.

When he heard a voice call out to him,

he was not sure if it was an actual person he was hearing or merely a fragment of a dream. He rubbed his sleepy eyes. They focused and then popped wide open as he realized this was not a dream at all. Not thirty feet away was a British naval warship, almost as huge as the *Grand Barnacle*.

"You there!" the ship's commodore called out to Jack from the forecastle of the naval vessel. "We have no record of your ship's registration. You are sailing unauthorized in British waters. Surrender now, or we will have no choice but to force you to do so—by any means necessary."

CHAPTER FIVE

"Gentlemen," Jack called out, "you're making a mistake. I am simply passing through these here waters. Just give me a brief moment and I'll be on my way."

"Surrender, now," the commodore called back. "And tell your captain and crew to come out from below deck and surrender as well."

"Captain? Crew? Sirs, I *am* the captain, and I *have* no crew," Jack replied.

The Royal Navy crew laughed condescendingly.

"Look, gents," Jack said, "This is all one big misunderstanding—"

"It is *you* who misunderstands," the commodore hollered back, cutting Jack off. "We are commandeering your ship. And once we do, you, and the crew and commander you are harboring, will answer a number of questions for us."

Jack laughed and threw up his arms. "Questions? What *questions* could you *possibly* have for *me*?"

The commodore shouted back, "Only the obvious ones: how did it come to be that the greatest warship ever to sail the Caribbean escaped notice until now? Where did said warship, unknown to the Royal Navy, and, worse, the Crown, come from? How could a boy as scrawny and frail as yourself *possibly* be sailing a ship like this on his own?" He added an even sharper note of condescension to his last question.

"Boy? Scrawny? Frail??? *What*!?" Jack shouted indignantly, looking down self-consciously at his lean chest.

"Men," the commodore continued, "prepare to board this ship. And take no prisoners."

Jack sighed and rolled his eyes. "I have told you already, there is no one on this ship but 'the boy,' however 'scrawny and frail' he might be!"

"No time for tall tales," the commodore shouted. "We're coming aboard."

Jack felt a sudden burst of anger erupt inside him. He straightened his back. "I am warning you, men, do not attempt to board this ship."

"Have you noticed that our cannons are

pointed right at your starboard?" the commodore asked.

"Hard not to, mate," Jack answered evenly.

"And that if by some stretch of the wildest imagination you *are* telling the truth, our men outnumber yours hundreds to one?"

"Noticed that, too."

"Well, then, help us aboard and surrender peacefully."

"I am warning you one last time," Jack said, gritting his teeth.

"Aim!" the commodore shouted as his men cocked their rifles.

Jack saw what was coming. He raised an eyebrow, then gasped and ducked below the *Grand Barnacle*'s railing for cover.

"Fire!"

A series of huge explosions rattled the *Grand Barnacle*. Smoke filled the air as a barrage of rifle fire hit the broadside of Jack's ship. Jack peeked over the balustrade cautiously. All he could see were plumes of white smoke flashing a fiery orange at irregular blast intervals. Then he realized the blasts weren't only coming from the naval ship, but from the *Grand Barnacle* returning fire as well. The Sword was glowing again. It must have been causing the *Grand Barnacle* to fire on the adjoining warship. The navy ship had moved closer now, close enough for the officers to stage their attack and board Jack's vessel.

Jack looked up and saw navy crewmen swinging from their ship onto the *Grand Barnacle*. In a panic, Jack grabbed the Sword and pointed it toward the men. Midway through the air, the men were transformed by a blinding flash. Instead of men, small octopuses and starfish now clung to the lines. They hung there a moment before tumbling into the sea.

"Oh, boy," Jack said worriedly.

Shrouded in smoke, the naval officers on the ship could not see what had happened to their seamen. And so they continued the battle, firing off cannons, rifles, and anything else they could find. Jack could hear screams and hollers, and he knew that whatever was happening was not good at all.

Suddenly there was a tremendous sound, like an entire forest of trees falling before thousands of axes. Then a great plume of smoke rose over the deck. Jack felt the cannons blast below him. He struggled to steady himself as the jolts rattled the deck. A painful ripping sound resounded over the ocean, accompanied by screams and moans. This awful noise was followed by silence.

Jack slowly crawled to the prow and

peered over. The thick smoke was beginning to dissipate. Jack found it difficult to breathe. He couldn't stop coughing for the gunpowder that hung in the air around him. But the sea breezes soon carried the smoke away, revealing a horrifying sight. All that was left of the navy ship was splintered timber and some remnants of the sails in the water before him.

"No," Jack cried. "No, no, *no*! This can't be happening!"

Jack waved the Sword frantically toward the area where the navy ship had been, trying to raise it from the depths. But nothing happened. He stared in disbelief as splintered planks bobbed on the waves. But it was no use. The ship had gone to Davy Jones's locker.

Stunned, Jack held his head in his hands for a moment. Then, he quickly jumped up.

In a furious panic, he began to race around the *Grand Barnacle*, examining it for damage. The ship had been rocked by explosions during the battle. But as Jack surveyed the ship, he didn't find a gash, a dent, or even a scratch on it. The Sword had protected the *Grand Barnacle*, and Jack with it.

Even for Jack, who was famous for taking things in stride, this was overwhelming. And, more important, it changed *everything*.

"Now, listen here," he said to the Sword through clenched teeth. "I've had as much as I can take of this. I am going to continue on this mission and retrieve my stone eye. Being that so many people—and nonpeople—want to get their hands on it, it must be worth something. Plus with all the mysterious pieces to your puzzle—scabbards, incantations—how do I know I don't need it to cement your power? Then, I am going to learn to use that power. Really use it. And once I do, we're going to use your power to free my mates from that snow-covered isle. And I will also use your power to heal my dying sailor! And then, we're going to send that decrepit, smelly old half-dead owner of yours back to whatever grave he crawled out of. Savvy?"

Jack raised his chin proudly and set the Sword back in its sheath.

As he did, the *Grand Barnacle* began to rock. Jack was tossed from one end of the deck to the other.

"Is there not a moment's rest here?" Jack asked, exasperated.

The waves became fierce, and a bone-chilling mist gathered around the boat. He knew then what was happening, and he smiled.

The mist thickened. There was a great

explosion that sent a roaring sound over the sea. Waves sprayed over the deck. Then the water settled, the mist began to lift, and under the light of the dying sun, the silhouette of Isla Sirena appeared on the horizon.

CHAPTER SIX

Jack pointed the Sword at Isla Sirena, and the *Grand Barnacle* raced toward it. He tried not to think about what had just happened to the Royal Navy vessel. But with the Sword doing the work of captain and crew there was little left for Jack to do *but* think. The event played in his mind over and over again. It seemed like a terrible dream that had left him with an uneasy feeling during his waking hours. He hoped, for the sake of the soldiers aboard the ship, that Davy Jones's locker was not nearly as terrible as the tales made it out to be.

Jack felt a jolt as the *Grand Barnacle* came to an abrupt halt. He was still almost a mile away from the shores of Isla Sirena. He peered over the side of the ship and noticed dark patterns in the water. The ship was snared on a huge reef.

"*Now* what?" Jack said.

"Jack Sparrow," a whispery voice called out, wafting over the ocean.

Jack looked around with a mix of confusion, suspicion, and caution.

"Jack Sparrow," came the voice again. It was clearly female.

Jack looked over the prow. Still no sign of the merfolk. But he knew they were here. All they needed to do was show themselves.

"Come on, Scaly Tails!" Jack shouted. "Come out and play!"

"Captain!" a new voice called out. This one was deeper.

"Jack!" still another voice cried. This one sounded very familiar.

"Bell?" Jack asked.

"Jack, help us. Come back. We need you," a voice that sounded just like Arabella's rang out over the waves.

Jack had encountered the merfolk before. He knew their games.

"Stop it, Scaly Tails, I'm on to you."

"But, Jack, I care for you. We all care for you," the voice that sounded like Arabella's said, tauntingly.

Jack was getting angrier.

"Jack . . ." Two new voices sailed over the waves.

"Tumen? Jean?"

Then more voices joined them. They called Jack's name over and over again. "Jack. Jack Sparrow. *Captain* Jack Sparrow . . ."

"Stop it!" Jack shouted, holding his ears. "Stop it right now!"

The voices stopped suddenly.

"Ah, that's better," Jack said, smiling.

But then the water around the ship began to splash and turn. Suddenly mermaids shot up from the depths, surrounding the *Grand Barnacle*. One after another they emerged from the sea. In a few seconds, there were a hundred of them. Then five hundred. And then, before he even knew what was happening, thousands of mermaids had surrounded the *Grand Barnacle*. And they all had one thing in common.

"Green-tails," Jack said soberly.

The Green-tails, Jack had learned, were the military arm of mermaid society. If they had a nasty bark, their bite was worse. Jack had the tooth-mark scars to prove it.

Jack could not get away even if he wanted to now. The ship was completely blockaded by the Green-tails. Unless . . . Jack thought for a moment about using the Sword. But after what had just happened with the navy ship, he thought the better of it. He did not want any more blood on his hands.

"I'll only use that blasted thing when I really need to," he said.

Besides, he was here to turn himself in, not to stage an attack. What could the Green-tail army do? Rip him to shreds a piece at a time?

On second thought, maybe they could. He preferred not to think about it.

"Good day, Scaly Tails," Jack said, placing his hand over his heart and bowing. "I have come to see your Blue-tail leaders, whose

names I have never had the fortune to learn. Can one of you—or better yet, *all* of you—go run and let them know I'm here for my appointment?"

"Jack Sparrow," one of the Green-tails hissed, "*you* will be brought to the chair-women. They will not be brought to you."

"Ah, '*chair*women.' One step closer to knowing their names now. Funny choice of title, though, you know, being they have no legs and could never possibly sit . . ."

"Silence!" The Green-tails said, their voices echoing over the sea.

"Okay, okay, no need to get all hissy . . ."

"Step from your vessel now," they commanded.

Jack shrugged. He had little choice. He lowered the gangplank the only way he knew how—by using the Sword—and descended into the mermaid-filled water. Toward the bottom of the plank, mermaids latched onto his ankles and began to drag him down into the sea.

Jack was underwater for what felt like only seconds before he emerged in a long cavernous tunnel that was filled with water up to his neck.

"Funny how this place works," Jack said. "One second you're only feet below the water, and the next you're in a corridor filled with air." He wasn't sure he'd ever get used to stuff like this.

The Green-tails ignored him. They escorted him toward the well-lit chamber at the end of the tunnel. As he approached, Jack recognized it as the chamber where the chairwomen held court. Sure enough, when he entered, the three Blue-tails were lying upon their thrones, their tails flicking.

"Jack Sparrow," the three mermaids said in unison.

"You know, I'm getting pretty sick of hearing my name over and over and over," Jack said.

"You have come to submit to us, yes?" the Blue-tail on the center throne asked.

"Well, sort of," Jack answered.

The Blue-tails shot him an angry glare.

"Kind of?" Jack said, shifting uncomfortably.

The mermaids' tails all flicked faster.

"Well, okay, yes. Yes I have," Jack said, dropping his head to acknowledge defeat.

The Blue-tails smiled, and their pointy teeth gnashed as they laughed. Then, the Blue-tail seated on the right noticed the Sword at Jack's side and her eyes widened. "Morveren," she said to the Blue-tail who sat in the center.

"Ah! Your name is Morveren!" Jack

shouted to the mermaid in the center, elated. Then he frowned. "Funny, I thought you looked more like a Susan."

The Blue-tails ignored him and continued their discussion.

"Morveren, the Sword."

Morveren nodded. "Jack Sparrow," she said, "we will bring you *and* your sword to your chamber now. Come."

"Now, wait a minute," Jack protested. "You have something of mine that I'd like back first. The collateral I left with you last time I visited your cozy home. You know what I'm talking about. Little round stone? Sort of looks like an eye?"

"Your collateral will not be returned to you until you are safely confined. Only then will you have submitted to us your greatest treasure. By our agreement, you owe us your freedom," Morveren said.

"And by the rules of collateral," the other two Blue-tails hissed in unison, "you must pay your debt in full before the object is returned."

"Now that's not exactly fair," Jack said. "I believe there must be something we can work out here. Let's make a deal."

"Very well," Morveren said. "We will accept the Sword. If you give it to us, you may keep your freedom. Otherwise, you keep the sword, and you are both imprisoned here."

Jack knew he still needed the power of the cursed Sword in order to save his crew and to defeat Cortés. Yet the stone eye was looking more attractive than ever to him, since everyone else seemed to want it. Which should he choose—stone or sword?

"I have a better idea," Jack said, thinking fast. "I propose a duel. If I win, I go free, with my sword *and* with my stone. If I lose, I stay here with you for eternity, you get to keep the eye, and the Sword is yours, too."

The three Blue-tails all whispered to one another.

"We find this a fair bargain," Morveren said.

"Yes," the others hissed.

"Prepare the battle chamber," Morveren shouted.

Half a dozen Red-tails, the servants of merfolk society who were always wading around waiting for orders, made their way to the far end of the chamber. They gripped heavy chains at either end of a huge iron gate. As they pulled, the gate lifted, revealing a wide alcove.

"You mean, I have to go in *there*?" Jack asked. But before he could say more, the

Red-tails were guiding him through the waist-high water. Once he was inside the alcove, the iron latticework gate crashed down, sealing the area off. Jack was trapped.

"Are you lot not playing fair again?" Jack shouted to the mermaids on the other side of the gate. "You said I could duel for my freedom."

"Oh, you can," Morveren said. "But we never said who—or what—you would be dueling."

With that, Jack heard a fierce rumbling in the enclosed chamber. At the far end of the alcove he saw two huge, glowing yellow eyes.

"Oh, no."

Then from the opposite side, in a dark cavernous part of the cell, he heard heavy footsteps—like an elephant's might sound—coming right toward him. The second creature stepped out from the shadows just enough that Jack could see its yellow eyes, too. It roared, baring huge razorlike teeth.

"This is not good," Jack said.

But at least he still had the Sword.

The beasts moved toward him.

Now Jack could see them clearly. They looked like iguanas. But they were much, much larger, with much sharper claws and much more powerful teeth!

Gripping his sword, Jack backed away from the terrifying figures.

"One more thing, Jack Sparrow," Morveren said. "That sword in your hands is powerless against creatures who reside in Davy Jones's locker—including your opponents."

The three Blue-tails smiled, then addressed Jack in unison. "Good luck, Jack Sparrow."

CHAPTER SEVEN

Jack looked at the closed gate behind him. Then he looked to either side of him. The only place he couldn't bring himself to look was dead ahead. The creatures were there, and they looked hungry. Their growls rang out like the roars of jaguars, echoing in the cavernous chamber.

Finally, Jack was forced to face the creatures as they lunged forward to attack. One of the beasts took a quick swipe at Jack, just missing him.

Jack examined his arm to make sure it was still attached to the rest of his body.

"Can't we act like civilized beasties?" he asked them.

The beasts roared.

"Guess not."

Jack sprang forward brandishing the Sword. Even though its mystical powers wouldn't work against the creatures, it still had a sharp blade. If Jack could steady his hand well enough to take aim, he'd have the beasts down in no time.

But landing the Sword on a slithering creature was not easy, and Jack was having difficulty even coming close. The beasts, on the other hand, had little problem cornering Jack.

Jack jumped back, escaping just in time as one of the beasts clawed at his legs. Jack had to come up with a plan. He couldn't keep darting around simply to stay alive. It wouldn't be long before he grew tired and fell prey to the two slobbering creatures.

As the two beasts closed in on him from either side, he sprang out from between them to the far end of the cell. They slammed their heads together and roared.

"Aha!" Jack shouted. "That's it!"

"Come and get me, beasties," Jack called, luring the beasts to the center of the chamber.

The creatures stalked over. As they sprang at him, Jack nimbly leaped from their paths. The beasts slammed into each other once again, this time with such force that they bounced off and hit the floor. Wearily, they made their way back to their feet.

They turned their attention to Jack once more. The beast to his right was crouched on its haunches, ready to pounce. The one on his left had its maw opened wide, prepared to devour Jack whole.

"If this doesn't work out, know that it was not very nice knowing you, mates," Jack said to the beasts.

Taking a deep breath, Jack vaulted off a nearby boulder and threw himself toward the openmouthed monster. The other beast ran stealthily after him. But, just before both creatures came down on him, the nimble sailor jumped out of their paths. The two beasts fell upon each other clawing and tearing. In fact, it looked as if they had forgotten all about Jack. Before long, the battle was over. The beasts had finished each other off, and Jack was victorious.

Jack wiped his hands and smiled. He calmly walked over to the chamber gate.

"Well, that's sorted out now, isn't it?" he said to his captors.

Morveren did not look pleased. Her expression turned from disappointment to resignation. She nodded to the Red-tails, who pulled on the heavy chains and raised the gate.

"Thanks, lasses," Jack said smoothly, winking at them.

Jack stepped before the three Blue-tailed mermaids and turned to Morveren.

"Now, where were we?" Jack said, "Oh, yes, you were about to let me leave here with my sword, my freedom, and my stone."

"We are bound by our agreement. You have won these things fairly, and so you are free to leave. You may take the Sword," Morveren said.

"Wonderful! And my stone eye?" Jack asked.

"That item is being held by Tia Dalma," Morveren said.

"Excuse me? Come again? *Pardon moi?*"

"We are no longer in possession of the eye. It is with the great mystic Tia Dalma, in her shack on the Pantano River," Morveren said. "To retrieve it, you must go there."

"And she'll just hand it over? Just like that?"

"She will abide by the rules of this fair duel. That is all we will say," the mermaid at Morveren's right said. "Tell her you were sent by Morveren, Aquala, and Aquila, and that the stone is yours by right. She has ways of knowing this is true."

"Let me guess," Jack said, pointing to the mermaid at Morveren's right, who had the distinction of a pair of wings growing from her back. "You're Aquala, and your friend over there is Aquila."

"Incorrect," she hissed. "I am Aquila."

"Yes, well, to-*may*-toe, to-*mah*-toe . . ." Jack said.

The mermaids were not amused.

The three chairwomen glared at Jack. It was clear they'd had enough of him.

"Leave at once," Morveren said.

"Very well, if you insist. I will reluctantly leave this lair where I was almost killed by raging beasties and nearly taken prisoner for the rest of my mortal days. Yes, it will be *very* difficult to leave," Jack said sarcastically. "Now, would someone be kind enough to show me out? And, if possible, can we take a back exit or something? Not to be rude, but that tunnel I came in by is a little dilapidated and unceremonious."

"You don't need us to show you the way," all three Blue-tails hissed. Aquila motioned to the Sword.

"Ah, right," Jack said. He lifted the Sword above his head and looked around cautiously. All eyes were on him. He had to make this work. Without hesitation, he conjured up the most powerful wish he could think of.

"Remove me from these Scaly Tail freaks presently!"

To Jack's amazement, the room began to glow. It became brighter and brighter, until Jack was enveloped in a sea of light too bright for his eyes. He shut them tightly against the glare. When he opened them again, he was back aboard the *Grand Barnacle*. Looking around, Jack realized the ship was sailing toward a familiar place: the mouth of the Pantano River.

He took a deep breath. He never liked going to see Tia Dalma, but he knew that he had no choice if he wanted to return to Isla Fortuna with everything he might need to save his crew. And he was beginning to realize that the stone eye might have a crucial role in any power play he'd be engaging in.

He climbed aboard one of the *Grand Barnacle*'s longboats and waved the Sword. With the help of the Sword's power, the boat fell softly onto the water. Then Jack began to row up the swampy terrain toward Tia Dalma's shack.

CHAPTER EIGHT

"Jack Sparrow," Tia Dalma said, welcoming him to her home. "What do you have for me?" She was a beautiful woman of the islands, who spoke with a Caribbean accent.

Jack climbed out of his longboat and onto Tia Dalma's porch, which was surrounded by swamp water. Because he didn't have any payment, which Jack knew she would request, he tried to steer the conversation in another direction.

"What, no 'Hello. How are you? Been a long time'?" he asked.

"Come inside," Tia Dalma said.

Jack stepped into the candlelit shack. It was filled all over with jars of herbs and spices, bottles full of potions, caged animals, bones—everything the greatest mystic in the Caribbean could need.

Tia Dalma stared at Jack with her wild eyes, and she smiled when she saw the Sword.

"I see you've gotten yourself into a mess again, have you?" Tia Dalma said. "The word on the winds is that you are drowning."

"Drowning?" Jack asked. "No, no, there's no drowning going on here. I was always a good swimmer," he said, placing a hand on the Sword.

"You can drown in things other than water. The Sword is full of power that is most difficult to balance, Jack Sparrow." As she spoke, she moved about her shack, arranging curiosities and petting a kind of animal that Jack had never seen before.

"Well, I have no choice. There are things I need to do with it."

"The waves say it has done things already. Have those things not been enough?" Tia Dalma asked.

Jack was silent for a moment, thinking about all the things the Sword had done. It was supposed to have been his greatest treasure. It was supposed to have granted him freedom. And yet all it had accomplished was alienating him from his crew and enslaving him to the will of Cortés.

"Look, I'm here because Morveren, Aquila, and Aquala sent me," Jack said. "They gave you something that was not theirs to give—being that it was actually *mine*—and I want it back."

Tia Dalma sighed, walked over to a shelf, and lifted a small bottle containing a greenish liquid. She filled a bowl with water and placed a drop of the green stuff into the bowl. She stared into the bowl briefly and then turned to Jack.

"It is so," she said, standing up and walking toward the rear of the shack. Presumably to retrieve the eye, Jack thought.

"The one you left has been looking for you," Tia Dalma said while she gracefully searched her canisters and containers.

"Oh, *everyone's* looking for me, love," Jack winked.

"But it is not all of them that you want to avoid—and the one I speak of is one who you do."

"Can't you ever just state something clear- and concise-like?" Jack asked.

Tia Dalma smiled. "Just be warned him

came here looking for you. Him wants him ring back."

Jack gasped. Now he knew who she was talking about. And it was someone Jack really did not want to see. In fact, it was someone he had been running from for a while. Talking about it was giving him a knot in his stomach. He once again decided to change the subject, though he knew Tia Dalma would eventually turn the conversation back to a difficult topic of some sort or other.

"So, this mate I'm sailing with says you turned his sister into a cat. Is it true?" Jack asked.

"You sail with a powerful crew, Jack Sparrow," Tia Dalma said, clearly evading Jack's question. "Do they know you are here?"

"I've not even told them I *know* you. Kept

it quiet, actually even pretended on a few occasions that I *didn't* know you," Jack said.

"Wise. But they have proven worthy. They will convene here soon," Tia Dalma said. To Jack it seemed this was both a request and a statement of fact.

"Yes, yes, of course. Now, where is my Stone-Eyed Sam–eye-stone-thing?" Jack asked, growing impatient.

"You know I demand payment," Tia Dalma said, smiling widely and staring at the Sword. "Even for this stone, which you say is yours."

"You want *this* here thing?" Jack asked, motioning to the Sword. "No, no, no, you don't want this. It's rather useless. Hardly works."

"I will accept no other payment," Tia Dalma said, crossing her arms.

"There is a minor complication," Jack

said. "I need it to save the crew you want to so badly meet."

Tia Dalma was clearly becoming annoyed. She walked to her table and slammed a bucket of crab claws down on it.

"Sorry, love, not very hungry right now," Jack said.

Tia Dalma shot Jack a warning glance and poured the claws onto the tabletop. She arranged them in different configurations. Jack knew then that she was reading a message in them. Once she had received a satisfying answer, Tia Dalma sighed. She walked back to Jack and handed him the stone eye.

"You will give me fair payment," she said, "when you have done all you set out to do and learned all you were meant to learn. This I cannot interfere with. This stone holds great power—greater even than that of the Sword. But its power is not easily unlocked. The stone itself is locked. It is a prison cell far smaller than any you have ever known."

Jack's head was reeling and, as he often did, Jack looked at Tia Dalma as if she were crazy. In truth, he knew she was anything but. She just spoke in a way that needed to be decoded.

"You will need these." She handed Jack two beads, one white and one red. "When you are ready to unleash the power of this eye—and only at that time—know it is red over white. And they *must* be tied to your person. Do this all and hold the eye. Only when you are ready, only when you know you *need* to. No sooner."

Jack placed the beads in separate pockets of his vest, just to make sure they wouldn't accidentally catch on a thread and touch, thereby unleashing the stone's power—

whatever that power might be. As unlikely as that seemed, Jack didn't want to risk it.

"Thank you, milady," Jack said, bowing. He moved to leave, but Tia Dalma grabbed his arm.

"Do not be fooled. Do not be arrogant. You are not safe yet, Jack Sparrow," she said, looking him in the eyes. She stared at him a moment and raised her eyebrows warningly.

"Very well," Jack said uncomfortably. "I will be seeing you soon."

"Yes," Tia Dalma said, "you will, surely. And you will bring with you my payment."

Jack grimaced.

"Take this as a parting gift," Tia Dalma said, handing Jack a bundle of dried herbs.

"What is it?" Jack asked.

"A rare magical herb called catnip," Tia Dalma answered. "It can undo what it has done. And it can redo what it has undone," Tia Dalma said, winking.

Jack smiled, then quickly left Tia Dalma's shack. He jumped into his longboat and rowed toward the *Grand Barnacle*, at the mouth of the river.

CHAPTER NINE

In what seemed like no time at all, Jack was again in sight of the shores of Isla Fortuna. The island was a sight to behold. From a mile away at sea, Jack could see the sandy beaches and tall palms covered in a thick blanket of snow. The sun shone brightly on the surrounding sea, but over the island hung a thick covering of gray clouds. The snow was still falling heavily, and drifts blanketed the sand dunes.

The small town of Puerto San Judas was still empty of people. Only the small inn near the town square was active. A thick plume of smoke billowed from the chimney. Jack knew his crew was still holed up in there. He also knew that apart from his crew there was at least one other soul upon the island—the phantom of Cortés himself. Jack wondered if Cortés was still standing upon the hilltop cemetery where Jack had left him.

Jack pointed the Sword at the island, "Land ho, mate!" he shouted, and the ship sped into port, docking beautifully.

"Couldn't have done it better myself," Jack said to the Sword. He gripped the eye of Stone-Eyed Sam in his left hand and wrapped his fingers around the hilt of the Sword of Cortés with his right.

"Ready or not, here I come," Jack said, less

confidently than he would have liked.

He tapped the gangplank with the Sword, and it was lowered onto the dock. As he descended the ramp, Arabella, Jean, and Fitzwilliam ran toward the boat. Arabella and Jean had wrapped themselves in blankets to keep warm. Fitzwilliam was wearing a fine coat. Jack could never figure out how that boy's clothes stayed so pristine, and how he managed to look dapper even in the most severe circumstances.

"Jack!" Arabella called out. "It's been days! Where have ye been?"

"Days, lass?" Jack asked sincerely. "Felt like no more than a few hours."

"It has been all we could do just to keep warm. You took the only boat in port, so we could not even sail to the warm ocean just one hundred feet offshore. We have been subsisting on scraps of food left here by the people of this island before they vanished." Fitzwilliam said.

"And Tumen's condition has worsened," Arabella told him.

"Jack," Jean said somberly, "we don't think he's going to make it."

Jack shook his head. "Oh, ye of little faith!" he said confidently. "I have all the power of the Caribbean here in my hands. We'll fix everything right away, including this nasty weather," he said dusting some snow off his shirt.

"With all due respect, 'Captain,'" Fitzwilliam said sarcastically, "that does not address the situation at hand. What good is all the power in the *universe*, if your crew is starving, freezing, and dying? Were it not for the fire at the inn, we would already be dead. Caribbean structures were not meant for this kind of weather."

"Oh, come on," Jack said, clearly frustrated. "Let us go to the inn and heal the poor chap. Then I'll go conquer Cortés, and we'll be off this island, with the Sword, in no time at all. . . ."

The others rushed back to the inn, and Jack followed close behind.

Inside, a huge fire was keeping the room at a comfortable temperature. But the specter of illness and—Jack hated to think it—death hung over the room.

"Tumen, lad!" Jack shouted, smiling.

Tumen was wheezing heavily, and could barely lift his head. Jack sat beside him casually, with one leg bent and the other stretched out. "Look, mate," Jack said, "I've got the Sword here. I am getting better at using it, and I can fix you so you're right as rain. Just give me a second," Jack said, standing up beside Tumen and flailing his hands theatrically as if he were casting a mystical incantation.

Jack pulled the Sword from its scabbard and waved it over Tumen.

But Tumen's response was not what Jack had anticipated. Instead of moaning a sigh of relief, jumping up, and thanking Jack for saving him, Tumen began to cough violently.

Arabella stood near the corner of the room, holding her hand over her mouth, choking back tears. Fitzwilliam stood nearby, his arms folded and his legs planted firmly apart, glaring angrily at Jack.

"We could have taken him away from this cursed island to a place where he could have recovered," Fitzwilliam said. "Instead, you sailed off for who knows what reason, while the chap laid here suffering."

Jack was getting angry. He was not sure if

he was angry at himself, at Cortés, or at the Sword, but he decided to take it out on Fitzwilliam. He pointed the Sword at the aristocrat.

"Listen here, mate, I've had about enough of you and your mouthing off," Jack said. "Now back off and I'll take care of this. Savvy?"

Fitzwilliam did not respond. Jean's mouth was quivering and he was no longer able to hold back his tears. Constance mewed pitifully by Tumen's side.

Jack did his magical-incantation-hand-thing again and waved the Sword over Tumen once more. This time, Tumen screamed in agony.

It was clear that the Sword was having a negative impact on him. Jack was beginning to realize that it was the Sword or Cortés, or a combination of the two, that had made Tumen sick in the first place. Jean ran to Arabella and clutched at her for comfort. Arabella held him close, trying to remain strong. Fitzwilliam's anger was welling.

"His blood will be on your hands," Fitzwilliam said to Jack.

"No," Jack said flatly. "His blood will be on no one's hands because he is going to be all right." He leaned in toward Tumen. "Did you hear me, mate? You're going to be all right," he said nervously. Fighting the urge to shed tears himself, he sprang up and ran toward the door.

"Jack, where are ye going?" Arabella asked.

"I am going to have a talk with the devil himself," Jack said.

"We are coming with you," Fitzwilliam said.

"No!" Jack shouted. "You are all staying here. Captain's orders."

Jack threw the door open and disappeared into the snow.

CHAPTER TEN

Jack stormed over to the snowy hillside cemetery where he had left Cortés before he set out to find the eye of Stone-Eyed Sam. Sure enough, Cortés was there, waiting for Jack's return. The conquistador was wearing the same evil smile that he had flashed at Jack before.

"You, there!" Jack called out.

Cortés did not move.

"You, Cortés, I'm back!" Jack said.

"I am not surprised," Cortés said. "With the power of the Sword at your side, there was little doubt in my mind that you would complete your mission."

"Yes, well, it wasn't just the Sword," Jack said. "In fact, my wiles proved a lot more beneficial to me than the Sword itself. The blasted thing didn't work against half the adversaries I faced, anyway. . . ."

Cortés was taken aback.

"You were in Davy Jones's lair?" Cortés asked, noting that those who come from Davy Jones's locker were the only beings who could not be affected by the Sword's power.

"Right you are!" Jack said.

Jack knew this wasn't entirely true. Isla Sirena moved back and forth from Davy Jones's locker to the surface world. It wasn't in Davy Jones's locker when Jack visited it.

At least, he didn't *think* it was. But saying he had been to Davy Jones's locker and back sounded impressive.

"Impossible," Cortés grumbled.

"No, actually it's not. And I'm living proof of it."

Cortés looked skeptical.

"So, you've brought back my stone, have you?" Cortés asked.

"I have brought back the stone, yes. But I beg to differ on whose stone it is. See, mate, I say it's mine. I won it fair and square not long ago on Isla Esquelitica," Jack said.*

Cortés's eyes glowed a deeper shade of red. "Give it to me," he demanded.

"Not till you do something for *me*," Jack said. "Now I know that sounds like a big

*Back in Vol I.: *The Coming Storm.*

favor to ask of you, who has done little or nothing for me since we've met. But think of all *I* did for *you*. You'd still be six feet under, or in an urn or a mausoleum somewhere if I didn't call you back from the dead." Jack smiled proudly. "So, I think you owe me one," he whispered to Cortés, trying not to lean in too closely to the putrid conquistador.

"What is your price?" Cortés asked, angrily.

"I want you to show me how to use this sword here," Jack said, tapping at the hilt of the Sword of Cortés. "Fully and completely. Savvy?"

Cortés laughed haughtily.

"Fool. You think this is all about you," Cortés said. "You think the power of the Sword was meant for the likes of you—you, who are little more than a bilge rat."

"I take offense to that," Jack said. "Were I a rat, I would certainly not reside in a bilge! I am a captain, after all."

"The power of the Sword is meant for me and for my purposes alone. I worried that a mind as sharp as yours would have figured that out by now. But it was also why I chose you over your little friends. You possess the wit, cunning, and grace to have retrieved the stone for me. And the stone is all I need to regain absolute power. Did you not notice that the Sword only worked in order to advance your goal—my goal, really—of procuring the stone?"

"I did notice that, in fact," Jack said. But, in truth, he had been so amazed by the Sword's power that he hadn't realized it till now. He had wanted the Sword because he thought it would give him freedom. But now he found that the Sword was enslaving him to Cortés. No matter what power the sword offered, no payoff was great enough for Jack to relinquish what he treasured most in the world—his freedom.

"I was not able to retrieve the eye myself," Cortés said, "because the seas are far too dangerous for me. Davy Jones wants the Sword, Tia Dalma would surely want to reign in my power, and the Aztec spirits are still bitterly opposed to me.

"But now, that will all change. With the Sword I will have godlike power, and with the stone eye, I will control the spirits, for they are contained in its confines. I will rule not only the Caribbean, but the Seven Seas!" Cortés shouted.

Jack suddenly understood what Tia Dalma meant when she said the eye was a prison. He laughed quietly, thinking how ridiculous it was that he had been carrying powerful spirits around in his pocket.

Then Jack heard someone call his name. He looked down the hill and saw Arabella running toward him.

"Jack! Ye must come quickly," she said, trying to catch her breath. "It's Tumen . . ." She trailed off, trying to compose herself.

She didn't need to say any more. Jack knew immediately what had happened. He had just lost his youngest crewmate. Tumen was gone.

CHAPTER ELEVEN

Jack was furious. After all he'd been through, he had not been able to save Tumen. Cortés sensed Jack's fury and laughed.

"You won't be laughing in a second, mate," Jack said threateningly.

"You're a fool, Jack Sparrow," Cortés replied. "You cannot defeat the dead."

"Oh, that's right, *I* can't," Jack said. Then he held up the stone eye, "But *this* can."

Cortés looked concerned.

"I've lied. That stone is good for nothing." Cortés laughed dismissively. But Jack could sense his nervousness.

"Then why do you want it so badly?" Jack asked.

Cortés was silent.

"Want it?" Jack teased, extending the stone out to Cortés. As Cortés reached out to grab the stone, Jack jerked it back. "Sorry, mate, I told you it's mine."

"Even if that stone had any sort of *power*, you would not know how to unleash it," Cortés said. "Just as you do not know how to use the power of the Sword."

"See, mate, that's where you're wrong," Jack said in a smart tone. He whipped out the two beads that Tia Dalma had given him.

Cortés stared at Jack condescendingly. "You think you can unleash any power the stone might have with those? What are they, anyway? Bits of rock? Pieces of candy? Bah!" Cortés cackled arrogantly.

"No, they were a gift from Tia Dalma."

Cortés's eyes grew wide at the name.

"And she taught me how to use them . . ." Jack began to twirl his long hair, until he had twisted several strands into one long lock. ". . . unlike you, who really didn't teach me a thing about how to use that dumb sword. You know, you really have to get your act together, Cortsy." Jack took the red bead and threaded it through the lock he'd made.

"You're going down, mate, and your cursed sword is going with you," Jack said to Cortés. He slipped the white bead onto the lock and knotted his hair at the end to hold the beads in place. Then he held the stone eye up to Cortés's decaying face.

Yet not even Jack was prepared for what happened next.

The instant the beads touched—red over white—the stone eye exploded. Streams of light burst from it like fireworks, whistling skyward. They expanded as they hit the air and dispersed in all directions, flying from the snowy island out over the Caribbean Sea and beyond.

"The spirits!" Cortés yelled.

They emerged from the small rock in what seemed like an endless flood, and they filled the sky like the aurora borealis. There was a moment of relative quiet, and then the loudest explosion yet rocked the island. From the fire and smoke emerged a spirit larger and more humanlike than all the others. The spirit faced Cortés, who looked disturbed.

"Montecuhzoma," Cortés mumbled.

"I see you two know each other," Jack said. He extended his hand to the spirit.

"Jack Sparrow here, mate. Very nice to meet you."

Montecuhzoma shot Jack a warning glance.

"All right, then," Jack said, stepping back. "Carry on."

"Cortés," the spirit said, "you disgraced me and my empire. Because of you I was stoned by my own subjects. Know now that I am here to retrieve the power you stole."

Arabella moved close to Jack and clung to him.

"Jack, do you know what's happening?" she asked.

"Well, the true fact of the matter is . . . I have not the slightest idea," Jack replied.

"I think Cortés called the spirit 'Monte-cuhzoma,'" Arabella said. "That's the word in Nahuatl, the Aztec language, for Monte-zuma—an emperor of the Aztec empire. He was subordinate to Cortés, thinking the conquistador was the god Quetzequotl. Even when Cortés began to destroy the traditions of the Aztec empire and massacred its people, Montecuhzoma did not relent in his support. Perhaps the Sword had something to do with his loyalty. In the end, Montecuhzoma was stoned with rocks and darts by his own people for urging them to retreat rather than to fight the Spaniards. Some say he died loyal to Cortés."

"Well, looks like that friendship didn't last terribly long in the afterlife," Jack said.

Jack felt a sudden tingle in his hand. The Sword was glowing again. And then it vanished . . . and reappeared moments later in Cortés's hand!

"That Sword held sway over me once," Montecuhzoma said. "Never will it again!"

Ignoring his warning, Cortés lunged

toward his opponent with the Sword drawn. Montecuhzoma lifted his hands and created an energy field, which blocked the Sword.

"Wow," Jack said in awe.

Montecuhzoma spread his arms and two Swords of Light appeared in his hands.

"I don't understand," Arabella said.

"Love, nothing has made much sense since we set sail from Tortuga."

"No, Montecuhzoma was also said to be a philosopher and a sage—not a warrior. He even took the throne reluctantly. So why is he fighting now?"

"Betrayal and death will do that to a fellow, I guess," Jack responded.

There was another explosion as Montecuhzoma and Cortés locked swords. Sparks of magical light and energy flew off the blades each time they clashed. And then Montecuhzoma made a decisive blow,

knocking the Sword from Cortés's hand. It flew to the ground, smoking with heat and melting the snow around it.

Arabella and Jack looked down at it. Jack reached down to retrieve it, but Arabella held him back.

"No, Jack, wait till this is through."

The two teenagers watched as Montecuhzoma gripped Cortés under his arms and lifted him in the air. Montecuhzoma suddenly took flight, leaving a trail of fire in his wake as he flew over the sea. Then he made a quick turn downward and plunged into the water with Cortés. The water steamed and boiled. Then there was silence.

Jack and Arabella watched in anticipation. At last, Montecuhzoma reemerged from the sea . . . without Cortés.

The spirit flew back toward the island, over Jack's and Arabella's heads. Finally, he hovered above the inn where Fitzwilliam and Jean were watching over Tumen. The spirit shone brightly, filling the space above and around the inn with light brighter than the sun. It was the brightest light Jack had ever seen. A moment later, the spirit flew off, northwestward.

Jack twisted the beads in his hair uncomfortably. He turned to Arabella, who expressed a look of shock.

"Bell, are you okay?" he asked her.

Then Arabella collapsed against Jack. As tough as she was, what had just transpired was far too much for her to bear. Still, Arabella began to wake almost immediately. Jack made sure she was all right, then bent down to pick up the Sword.

"Jack! What are ye doing?" Arabella cried out.

"Trust me, love. I've one more thing

to do with this blasted sword."

Jack eyed the Sword with grave disappointment. It had promised so much. It should have been his ticket to freedom. Instead, it, like its namesake, was just a despot that made anyone who wielded its power a pawn in its game.

Jack lifted the Sword in the air. With Cortés gone, he suspected it would obey him. It only had one master now.

"Now, mate," he said to the Sword, "undo anything you've done that would have helped your old master. Undo the things that would have pleased Cortés."

The town square lit up, and the confused citizens of Puerto San Judas reappeared. The docks were repaired and full of ships. Much to his disappointment, the *Grand Barnacle* had transformed back into the little fishing vessel Jack and his crew were used to.

"Would have been a chore to sail that thing, just the five of us, anyway," Jack said.

Jack looked out on the sea and noticed a familiar ship sailing near the horizon. It was the Royal Navy vessel the Sword had sunk out at sea. Jack heaved a sigh of relief. He wondered if the crew remembered anything of what had happened.

And there were certain things that strangely didn't change at all—the snow was still falling, though lightly now, over Isla Fortuna. And Left-Foot Louis and his crew, whom the Sword had conquered, did not reappear. Nor did Tumen.

Jack turned to Arabella, and they shared a moment of silence for their fallen crewmate.

Then, they heard a rush of footsteps coming up the hillside. They turned to see Fitzwilliam and Jean, followed by

Constance struggling in the snow. And behind them . . . Tumen!

"Oh, my stars," Arabella said, holding her hands to her mouth. Tears of joy and relief welled up in her eyes. The spirit of Montecuhzoma must have saved him. Arabella ran to Tumen and embraced him. Jack rushed over as well.

"You're all right, mate! See, I told you we'd make you right as rain!" Jack said. "So how was the other side?" he asked.

"Cold," Tumen responded.

Everyone laughed uncomfortably.

"Well, it couldn't be any colder than it is here," Jack said. "Let's sail out of here quickly, to somewhere . . . warm."

"Tumen wants to return home," Jean told them.

"Then it is off to the Yucatán! You never deny a man his un-dying wish," Jack said.

Jack gathered up the Sword and put it in its scabbard.

"What are ye going to do with that thing, Jack?" Arabella asked.

"There's someone to whom I owe a debt, and this is just the payment she will accept."

As they made their way through the town square, the residents of Puerto San Judas looked bewildered and puzzled. Children were joyfully building snowmen and tossing snowballs at one another.

"Well, this is odd," Jack said.

A finely dressed man approached the crew.

"You, there, strangers," he called out to them. "I am governor here, and demand you tell me who you are and what you know of what happened upon this island."

"What is the last thing you remember?" Jack asked.

The man shook his head confusedly, clearly straining to remember any detail he could.

"I don't remember anything," he said. "None of us does."

"Well, then," Jack said, smiling, "I guess nothing happened."

As the crew boarded the *Barnacle*, Jack leaned over the hull and shouted down at the townsfolk, "But you might want to consider changing the name of your dear home to Snowy Island. Better start chopping firewood!

"Crew," Jack shouted, "chart a course to the Yucatán."

"Aye, sir!" Jean said, saluting his captain.

"And remember," Jack continued, "I need to make a quick stop at the mouth of the Pantano River along the way."

Epilogue

"Jack Sparrow, you've come back. Not that I am surprised. The sea told me you would return with your fair payment. And you've brought guests," Tia Dalma said.

Jack and his crew sat in the mystic's shack. Jack was cool, as usual. The crew, on the other hand, was in awe.

Constance cowered in a corner, and Jean was antsy. After all, it was Tia Dalma who had turned Constance from Jean's sister into a cat!

Jack stepped up to the legendary mystic and presented her with the Sword.

"All yours, love," Jack said.

"The Sword belongs to no one," Tia Dalma corrected. "But I will house it here, and it will not be misused again."

"Madam, please, I beg your forgiveness, but, please, madam . . ." Jean said, stammering.

"The power to return your sister to her previous form lies in Jack Sparrow's hands now," Tia Dalma said, reading Jean's thoughts.

"What . . . but how?" Jean asked, looking back and forth between Jack and Tia Dalma.

Tia Dalma smiled.

"I have no bloody idea what she's talking about," Jack said. "And now," he continued, quickly changing the subject, "we must be going."

"Proceed carefully, Jack Sparrow," Tia Dalma said, showing Jack and his crew to the door. "You've already drunk a sip of what the sea has in store for you. And be warned, the Sword is not the only curse Cortés has left behind."

"No worries, love," Jack said as he and his crew left Tia Dalma's shack and boarded a longboat. "From now on, it's only uncursed treasure for us. Riches are a perfectly fine way to secure freedom. Savvy?"

"Jack Sparrow, don't play the fool," Tia Dalma said. "You know better than anyone on the Seven Seas that in the Caribbean, magic and treasure go hand in hand."

Tia Dalma smiled and winked at Jack. Then she quickly closed the door of her swampland shack behind them.

Don't miss the next volume in the continuing adventures of Jack Sparrow and the crew of the mighty Barnacle!

The Age of Bronze

With the Sword of Cortés ordeal over, Jack and his crew take a break in Tumen's village on the Yucatán peninsula. But when a powerful amulet goes missing from the village, Jack and his crew become the prime suspects. Can they clear their good names and conquer the mysterious duo they believe to be the real thieves?